THE GREAT ESCAPE

Ice Age 2: The Great Escape
Ice Age 2 The Meltdown™ & © 2006 Twentieth Century Fox Film Corporation.
All rights reserved.
Printed in the United States of America.
No part of this book may be used or reproduced in any manner whatsoever without written
permission except in the case of brief quotations embodied in critical articles and reviews.
For information address HarperCollins Children's Books, a division of HarperCollins
Publishers, 1350 Avenue of the Americas, New York, NY 10019.
www.harperchildrens.com
www.iceage2.com
Book design by John Sazaklis

Library of Congress catalog card number: 2005934266
ISBN-10: 0-06-083972-4—ISBN-13: 978-0-06-083972-7

❖
First Edition

ICE AGE 2 ™
THE MELTDOWN

THE GREAT ESCAPE

Adapted by Judy Katschke

Illustrated by Artful Doodlers, UK

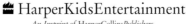

HarperKidsEntertainment

An Imprint of HarperCollins*Publishers*

CHAPTER ONE

"No running, James!" Sid warned. "Camp rules!"

The young aardvark looked back at Sid. "Bite me, Sloth!" he sneered.

Sid heaved a sigh.

He thought running his own camp would give him a little respect. But Campo del Sid was quickly turning into Campo del Brats!

Today the animal campers were chilling at the Glacier Water Park. Deep cracks in the glaciers made the best water slides. Icy puddles made awesome pools. It was the coolest place to come along in the whole Ice Age!

But Sid was not a happy camper.

"Jared, you just ate! Wait an hour before you go swimming!" Sid ordered. "Hector, stop picking your—Ahhhh!"

Sid flipped over. He looked up and gulped.

The campers had tied his tail to a tree branch!

"Piñata!" they shouted.

Sid saw stars as he got whacked with a club. One giant whack sent him tumbling to the ground.

"You don't have any candy in you!" a beaver camper complained.

The campers tossed Sid into a hole. They covered him halfway with dirt and bounced on his head.

"What's going on here?" a voice boomed.

Sid smiled with relief. His best buds Manny and Diego had stopped by.

The kids jumped off Sid as the huge woolly mammoth and saber-toothed tiger walked over. Manny used his long trunk to dig Sid out.

"I told you, Sid," Manny said. "You're not qualified to run a camp."

"You guys don't think I can do anything," Sid argued. "But these kids look up to me!"

Two little beavers tied Sid's legs together. They gave him a push and—*thump*—Sid fell flat on his face!

"Yeah, I can see that," Diego snorted.

Sid watched as Manny and Diego walked away. His friends were always on his case. But he would show them!

"If they can't appreciate me for my work with the kids," Sid muttered. "I've got bigger mountains to climb!"

Sid hopped away, his feet still tied together.

"Hey!" an aardvark said, pointing to Manny. "Let's play pin the tail on the mammoth next!"

Manny and Diego were about to yell for Sid when a loud rumbling noise filled the air. Hundreds of animals began running in all directions. One stepped on Manny's trunk as they stampeded by.

"Watch it!" Manny shouted.

"Where's everybody going?" Diego asked.

"Didn't you hear?" an animal called back. "The world is ending!"

Chapter Two

"Who says?" Manny demanded.

"Fast Tony," a running elk answered. "He said the whole world is going to flood!"

Fast Tony was a fast-talking armadillo. He was so slick he could sell snake oil to snakes. But that day Fast Tony and his Glyptodon assistant Stu were selling survival!

"Folks!" Fast Tony told a crowd of animals. "I hold in my hand a device that can pull air out of the sky!"

Fast Tony grinned at an aardvark lady. "Do you have gills, ma'am, so you can breathe underwater?" he asked.

"No," she answered.

"Let my assistant Stu demonstrate," Fast Tony said.

Stu pulled out two reeds. He stuck them up his nose and said, "Hey! I can smell the ocean!"

"You suck the air through your mouth, moron!" Fast Tony yelled. He jammed a reed into Stu's mouth.

Then he shoved Stu's head into a puddle. He held it there until Stu jumped up sputtering for air.

"Results may vary," Fast Tony said with a chuckle.

In a flash, Fast Tony was yanked off the ground. Glancing up, he saw two sharp tusks and a long mammoth trunk.

"Why are you scaring everyone with this doomsday stuff, Fast Tony?" Manny asked.

Fast Tony rolled up in a ball and bounced away from Manny.

"It's all part of my weather forecast," he said. "It calls for intense flooding followed by the end of the world."

The crowd gasped.

"Don't listen to him!" Manny said. "The world will always be covered with ice."

"Say, buddy," an aardvark dad shouted. "Haven't mammoths gone extinct? Aren't you the last of your kind?"

Manny rolled his eyes. Those ants the aardvark had been sucking must have gone straight to his brain.

"Mammoths can't go extinct!" Manny shouted back. "They're the biggest things on earth!"

"Dinosaurs were big," a beaver mom said. "And they're extinct."

"Dinosaurs made a lot of enemies," Manny said. He was about to explain when—

"Look!" a voice piped up. "Some idiot is going down the Eviscerator!" The Eviscerator was a huge slide made of ice.

Manny groaned.

"Please tell me that's not *our* idiot," he said.

Everyone looked all the way up. Standing on the peak of the glacial mountain slide was Sid.

"I'm going to jump on the count of three!" Sid shouted. But when he looked down his stomach flipped. There had to be a better way to get respect.

"Jump, jump, jump!" the crowd urged.

Manny and Diego didn't think Sid was stupid

enough to do it. But they had been wrong before.

"Get down from there, Sid!" Manny demanded, racing up to where Sid stood. Diego followed him.

"No way!" Sid shouted. "I'm going to be the first to jump off the Eviscerator. Then you guys are going to respect me!"

Sid squeezed his eyes shut. Then he yelled, "Geronimooooo!"

The crowd went wild as Sid began his plunge.

But just as Sid took off, he was snatched up by Manny, who slipped and fell backwards, knocking Diego onto a frozen lake behind them. Then the hefty mammoth crash-landed on top of Sid.

"I can't . . . breathe," Sid gasped.

The ice under Diego's feet began to crack. He couldn't breathe either, but only because he was so scared. He ran for shore, racing over the rapidly melting ice. When he reached the shoreline, he took a final leap and landed right on top of Manny.

"You know, if I didn't know better, Diego, I'd think you were afraid of the water," Sid said.

Diego grabbed Sid by his furry neck. No one called a saber-toothed tiger afraid and got away with it!

"Um . . . good thing I know you better," Sid said.

"Guys!" Manny cut in. "Fast Tony was right. Everything *is* melting!"

The friends watched wide-eyed as chunks of the iced-over lake collapsed into an enormous

sea. The only thing holding back the surge was the dam they were standing on.

"Maybe we can evolve into water creatures," Sid said. "Just call me . . . Squid!"

Manny knew a meltdown was serious business.

"It's all going to flood," Manny said. "We have to warn everybody!"

CHAPTER THREE

First, Manny, Sid, and Diego set out to warn the campers. They crossed over a long ice-bridge leading to the water park. The friends were halfway across when Sid shook his head.

"This bridge is a piece of junk," he said, breaking off a sliver of ice.

Manny and Diego stared at the icicle in Sid's hand.

"What?" Sid asked.

Crrrrrraaaaaaack!

The whole bridge crumbled. Manny, Sid, and Diego plunged down, screaming all the way. They flew over a gorge, shot across the water, and crashed down onto Fast Tony's platform.

"Look!" Fast Tony told the crowd. "Furry balls of lava raining from the sky!"

The crowd laughed.

Fast Tony had just told them about some giant

thing that floats. What would he try to sell them next—ice cubes?

"You've got to listen to Fast Tony," Manny told the animals. "He's right about the flood."

"I am?" Fast Tony gasped.

"We saw what's up there," Manny said. "When the dam breaks, we'll all be under water."

"So," Fast Tony said with a grin. "Who wants to buy directions to that giant thing that floats?"

Claws and paws shot up.

"You know what I like about you, Fast Tony?" Diego sneered. "You're crunchy on the outside and chewy on the inside!"

Fast Tony gulped as he eyed Diego's razor-sharp teeth. He turned to the crowd and said, "I meant the directions are free! The floating thing is at the far end of the valley!"

"I don't see anything!" a beaver complained.

"How do we know it's real?" a bison demanded.

"It's called a boat and it's real," a voice said. "I've seen it myself."

Heads turned to see a lone vulture leaning against a tree. His feathers were smooth—and so was his attitude.

"You'd better hurry," the vulture said. "Grounds are melting. Walls are tumbling. In three days' time—*boom!*"

The crowd jumped back.

"There *is* some good news," the vulture said. "The more of you that die, the better I eat!"

The vulture spread his wings and flew off.

"He must have been a pleasure to have in class," Sid snorted.

"Alright!" Manny announced. "You heard the scary vulture. Let's move out—"

Crash!

A monster of an ice boulder cracked off the dam and was plunging straight down toward the animals.

Everyone ran for safety. The giant boulder splashed down in the water park. As it bobbed in the water, Manny saw two dark shadows behind the frosty ice. He didn't know what they were. He just knew they were ugly.

"Manny, let's go!" Diego called.

Manny, Sid, and Diego joined the march to the boat. At the same time, something fishy was happening inside the boulder. Two prehistoric reptiles named Cretaceous and Maelstrom were waking up

after a long frozen sleep—one that had lasted a million years.

Cretaceous had a scaly, gatorlike snout and needle-sharp teeth. Maelstrom was a big bloated sea cow with amber eyes and flaring nostrils.

Nap time was over for them.

Now it was time for a little *snack*!

CHAPTER FOUR

"Keep it moving!" Manny said, using his trunk to direct traffic. Hundreds of mammals were marching toward the end of the valley and the boat.

"I just heard that you're going extinct, Manny," Sid said. "Can I have your spot on the food chain?"

"I am *not* going extinct!" Manny cried.

An aardvark dad pointed to Manny. "Look, kids," he said. "The last mammoth!"

"Whooooaaaa!" the little aardvarks gasped.

Manny, Sid, and Diego fell into step with the migration. Most of the animals were worried about their own survival. But Manny was starting to worry about the survival of his whole *species*!

Passing a forest, Manny gazed at his reflection in a hanging icicle.

"What if they're right?" Manny asked. "What if I

am the last mammoth?"

"You still have us!" Sid said cheerily.

"That's not a great argument," Diego growled.

Sid and Diego watched as their big hairy friend walked into the forest. Alone.

"One is the loneliest number." Sid sighed.

Just then—

Whack! Whack!

Pebbles rained down on top of Sid and Diego.

"Ow!" Sid cried.

"Who did that?" Diego demanded.

There was only one way to find out.

Diego and Sid charged into the forest. Two possums were hanging from a tree by their tails. Their names were Crash and Eddie, and their weapon of choice was peashooters made out of reeds.

"These work great!" Crash said. He dropped a pebble into his reed, blew into it, and—

Whack!

He hit Diego again.

"Cool!" Eddie cried.

Diego howled. But before he could swipe his sharp claws at the possums, they dove into holes in the ground.

"Missed me!" Eddie taunted.

Sid and Diego didn't know where the possums would pop up next. They put up a good chase, but with their pebble shooters, the possums were armed and dangerously pesky.

"Gotcha!" Eddie cried, blasting another pebble.

The possums had a good laugh . . . until Diego crept up behind them and said, "Boo!"

"Waaaaaah!" the possums screamed.

Diego lunged at Crash and Eddie. They blasted the tiger with more pebbles before popping back in their holes.

Sid had had enough of this crazy game. He puffed out his scrawny chest and declared, "I'm going in!"

As Sid began to charge, Crash and Eddie hooked tails. Sid yelped as he tripped over the furry trip line.

Laughing, the possums scurried up a hill. Sid and Diego collapsed on the ground, exhausted.

"If anyone asks, there were fifty of them." Diego said. "And they were rattlesnakes."

Suddenly . . .

"Here, kitty, kitty!" Eddie called.

Diego snarled. Who was he calling *kitty*?

Diego charged up the hill.

"Retreat!" Crash shouted.

While the battle raged on, a woolly mammoth sat sadly on a riverbank. Manny stared at his reflection in the water and wondered, was he really the last of his kind?

The water rippled. Manny's image vanished,

and the reflection of two other mammoths appeared. They were Manny's wife and son, the family he had lost to hunters not too long ago. A tear filled Manny's eye as the reflection changed back to his own.

"It's just you and me now," Manny sighed.

Then he heard a branch snap. An enormous shape dropped down from a tree, but before hitting the ground, it stopped.

Manny's eyes popped wide open. Hanging upside down from a branch and looking straight at him was another mammoth!

CHAPTER FIVE

"Ahhhh!" Manny shouted, startled.

"Ahhhh!" the hanging mammoth shouted back.

The branch broke, sending the nine-ton mammoth crashing to the ground. Her name was Ellie. She was just as surprised to see Manny as he was to see her.

But the biggest surprise was yet to come.

"I knew I wasn't the only one!" Manny cheered.

"Me, too," Ellie said. "Everyone falls out of a tree now and then. They just don't admit it."

"What?" Manny asked. Since when did mammoths fall out of trees?

"Some of us have a hard time staying on branches," Ellie babbled on. "It's not like we're bats or something!"

"And you were in the tree *because*?" Manny asked slowly.

"I was looking for my brothers," Ellie said.

"Brothers?" Manny asked happily. "You mean there are more?"

"Sure," Ellie said. "There are lots of us."

"Where are they? Where are they?" Manny asked.

"Under rocks. In holes in the ground," Ellie said. "We like to come out at night so the birds don't carry us off."

"Huh?" Manny asked. Since when did birds carry off nine-ton mammoths?

A rustling noise interrupted Manny's thoughts, then the sound of someone yelling, "Help! Help!"

Crash and Eddie burst out of the bushes. Chasing them were Sid and Diego. When Sid saw Ellie, he screeched to a stop.

"Well, shave me down and call me a mole rat," Sid declared. "You found another mammoth!"

"Where?" Ellie asked. "I thought mammoths were extinct!"

Manny, Sid, and Diego stared at Ellie. If it looked like a mammoth . . . and walked like a mammoth . . . and talked like a mammoth—then it *was* a mammoth. Right?

"Why are you looking at me?" Ellie asked.

"Maybe because you're a mammoth?" Manny asked.

"Me?" Ellie laughed. "Don't be ridiculous. I'm not a mammoth. I'm a possum!"

"And I'm a newt," Manny joked. He pointed to Sid and Diego. "This is my friend the badger and my other friend the platypus."

Crash and Eddie walked over to Manny like a couple of tough guys.

"Is this guy bothering you, Sis?" Crash asked.

"Sis?" Manny, Sid, and Diego cried together.

"That's right," Ellie said. "I'm Ellie. These are my brothers, Crash and Eddie. We're all possums. See?"

Manny was dumbstruck. What part of mammoth didn't she get?

"I don't think her tree goes all the way up to the top branch," Manny whispered.

Just then Sid had a brainstorm.

"Hey!" he whispered. "If she's a mammoth she should come with us!"

"Are you crazy? No way!" Manny hissed.

"Okay," Sid said. He turned to Ellie and said, "Manny wants me to ask you if you'd like to escape the flood with us."

"No way!" Crash exclaimed.

"I'd rather be roadkill!" Eddie said.

"That can be arranged," Diego sneered.

Ellie whisked her brothers aside. "These guys can protect us out in the open," she whispered. "What do you say?"

The two possums and one possum-wannabe talked it over. Manny, Sid, and Diego talked it over, too—their own way.

"Ow!" Sid yelled as Manny swatted his head.

"Why did you invite them?" Manny demanded.

"Because you might be the last mammoth on earth!" Sid said.

"Sid has a point," Diego said. "This could be

your last chance to have a family."

Manny's heart ached as he remembered his wife and son. "I don't want another family," he said.

Ellie lumbered over. "My brothers and I gratefully accept your invitation to travel with you," she announced.

"*If* you treat us nicely," Crash said.

"Maybe we'll have a little snack for the road," Diego growled.

"You want a piece of us?" Eddie sneered.

The fur began to fly.

The sound of falling ice made everyone stop cold. They had forgotten why they were traveling in the first place—to escape the flood!

"We're going to travel together like one big happy family," Manny ordered. "So let's move it before the ground falls out from under our feet."

The travelers marched together. But the more they walked, the more Ellie played possum. When a hawk flew by she pretended to be dead.

"That hawk could have swooped down and snatched me up for dinner," Ellie said, shivering. "That's how Cousin Wilton went."

Manny groaned under his breath. How could he get it through her big woolly head that she was a *mammoth*?

"Ellie, look at our footprints," Manny pointed out. "They're the same shape. Look at our shadows. We match!"

Ellie studied the footprints and shadows. "They do match," she said. "You must be part possum!"

I give up! Manny thought.

The travelers journeyed on. They floated across a frozen lake on a giant ice floe. Diego gritted his sharp teeth as Crash and Eddie slid and glided on the ice.

"Will you cut it out?" Diego hissed. "Can't you see you're wearing the ice out?"

"It's strong enough to hold a ten-ton mammoth and a nine-ton possum," Sid pointed out.

But it was not enough to hold back an enormous prehistoric reptile as it came crashing through the ice.

The crew screamed as Maelstrom sent them all flying through the air.

"Mammal overboard!" Sid shouted as he landed in the water with a splash.

The others landed on smaller ice floes. Diego stiffened with fear as he gripped the ice with his claws.

Sid sloth-paddled to Diego's floe. When the terrified tiger wouldn't move, Sid leaned over and chomped on Diego's tail.

"*Yowwww!*" Diego howled.

It worked!

Diego chased Sid across the floe. They made it to shore just as Maelstrom chomped the last sliver of ice.

"What in the animal kingdom was that?" Sid asked.

But Maelstrom was not the only nasty creature in

the icy sea. Cretaceous leaped out of the water next to Manny's ice raft. With a snap of his long, pointed jaw he clamped down on Manny's tusks.

Manny shook Cretaceous off. The creature soared through the air before splashing back into the water.

The mammals gathered safely on shore. Manny glanced back at the reptiles.

Their huge, hungry mouths said nothing. But their eyes said, *We'll be back*!

CHAPTER SIX

"Wow, Manny," Ellie said. "Fighting off that creature was the bravest thing I ever saw!"

Manny blushed under his fur. "Oh, it was nothing—" he said.

"It's not a compliment," Ellie said. "To a possum, bravery is dumb."

"Dumb?" Manny asked.

"Maybe mammoths are going extinct because they put themselves in danger too often," Ellie explained. "Maybe you should run away more, like possums do."

Manny stared at Ellie as she walked away with her brothers. "Do you believe her?" he cried. "She's stubborn! And narrow-minded!"

"You like her!" Sid teased.

"I do not!" Manny said as he stomped away.

"Your secret is safe with me!" Sid called. He turned to Diego and said, "So is yours."

"What secret?" Diego demanded.

"The one about how you can't swim," Sid said. "You're going to have to face your fear sooner or later."

"What do you know about fear?" Diego demanded.

"Impossible as it may seem," Sid said, "sloths have natural enemies that would love to kill us."

"I wonder why," Diego growled.

"Most animals can swim as babies," Sid explained. "For a tiger, it's like crawling on your belly to stalk helpless prey."

Sid demonstrated. He lay across a log on his belly and stretched his arms and legs.

"Now claw, kick, claw, kick!" Sid said. "See? I'm stalking the prey!"

"That's ridiculous," Diego muttered.

Deep inside, Diego knew Sid was right. When it came to water, the fierce saber-toothed tiger was nothing more than a big scaredy-cat!

The mammals trudged on. When they climbed to the top of a hill, they found more logs.

"Let's roll!" Eddie shouted.

Crash and Eddie jumped inside the log. They spun around and around as it rolled down the hill.

Ellie was on a roll, too. She balanced on top of another log as it spun after her brothers. "Meet you on the other side!" she shouted.

The first log hit the bottom. Crash and Eddie jumped out and high-fived. Then Crash climbed to the top of a tall tree.

"Hey, Manny!" Crash called. "Can you pull back the tree and shoot me into the pond?"

Manny didn't want to do it. But he *did* want to impress Ellie. So he grabbed the tree with his trunk and pulled it way back.

"Farther," Crash called. "Farther . . . now!"

Manny let go. The tree snapped forward and flipped Crash through the air.

"I can fly!" Crash cheered. "I believe I can—"

Smash! Crash collided with another tree.

Ellie's log stopped just as her unconscious brother slid to the ground.

"What's wrong with you, Manny?" Ellie scolded.

Eddie cradled his brother in his arms. "Don't go, Crash!" he blubbered. "Who's going to watch my back? Who's going to roll in the dung patch with me?"

"Dung patch?" Crash's eyes popped open. He sprung to his feet and shouted, "I can stand! I can run!"

"It's a miracle!" Eddie shouted.

"Oh, well," Ellie sighed. "Boys will be boys."

Yeah, Manny thought. *And mammoths will be possums!*

The mammals marched on. The sun was setting just as they came to a forest. The trees were slanted, and the roots were exposed. It was the weirdest-looking forest most of them had ever seen. But to Ellie, it was magical.

"Ellie, where are you going?" Manny called.

Ellie didn't answer as she moved deeper into the forest. Manny found Ellie in a meadow filled with willow trees. The tops of the willows were shaped like mammoths.

"I know this place," Ellie said.

In her mind's eye she saw a baby mammoth running across a snowy meadow. The baby was cold, lost, and very alone—until she saw a long, skinny tail dangling from a tree. Looking up, the baby mammoth saw a smiling possum mom with her two tiny sons. No longer alone, the baby smiled.

Ellie snapped out of her flashback. The baby

mammoth was her!

A tear filled Ellie's eye as she studied her footprint. It was exactly the same shape as Manny's.

"A mammoth never forgets," Manny said softly, realizing what was going on.

"I always knew I was different," Ellie admitted. "I was a little bigger than the possum kids. Okay, a lot bigger!"

"There's nothing wrong with being big-boned," Manny said.

"Now I understand why possum boys never found me appealing," Ellie sighed.

"That's too bad," Manny blurted. "Because as far as mammoths go, you're . . . uh . . ."

"What?" Ellie asked.

"A-a-attractive," Manny stammered.

"That's sweet," Ellie said with a smile.

Manny smiled, too. He had finally admitted his crush on Ellie. And now that she knew she was a mammoth, he liked her even more.

Manny and Ellie walked side-by-side as the march went on. When they reached the base of a cliff, the crew was too tired to push through. They built a fire and one by one they curled up on the ice to sack out.

"Should we be resting?" Ellie asked. "Maybe we should keep walking."

"You're right," Manny said with a yawn. "We should . . . keep . . . walking . . ."

Manny let out a rumbling snore. He was out like a light.

Sid was already fast asleep on a rock by the fire. He thought he was dreaming when he felt the rock move . . .

CHAPTER SEVEN

"Huh?" Sid murmured as he woke up. He sat up and looked around. The rock was being carried by a whole army of mini-sloths!

"Um, can I help you?" Sid asked.

The mini-sloths didn't answer. As they reached a clearing in the woods, Sid saw a whole tribe of mini-sloths. They dropped to their knees and bowed down to Sid.

"Anyone speak sloth?" Sid asked.

Sid was lowered to the ground. He was handed two rocks. A mini-sloth pointed to a fifty-foot-high statue. Sid's mouth dropped open. The statue was of him!

"Fire-god!" the mini-sloth declared.

"Oh, so that's it!" Sid said. "I'm the Fire-god!"

Sid rubbed the rocks together. Sparks hit patches of bubbling tar, and flames exploded into the air.

The mini-sloths went wild as Sid kept the flames

coming. The misunderstood sloth felt like a rock star. Especially when the mini-sloths paraded him through the village on a vine-covered platform.

"Thank you! Thank you!" Sid cried. They didn't just respect him, they *worshipped* him. If only Manny and Diego could see him now!

Suddenly the platform stopped moving. Sid felt vines twisting around his body. He saw smoke rising before him.

"This is either very good," Sid said, "or very bad."

He looked down and gulped. Right below was a boiling, bubbling tar pit!

"Why kill Fire-god?" Sid cried. "A thousand years' bad juju for killing Fire-god."

"Superheated rock from the earth's core is rising to the top," a mini-sloth explained. "The ice is melting and causing a great flood."

"We can find a solution together," Sid pleaded.

"We have one," the mini-sloth said. "Sacrifice the Fire-god."

The platform tipped. Sid screamed as he fell toward the burning pit. Soon he would go from being Fire-god to crispy critter.

A vine snagged on an outcropping of rock, and Sid bounced up and down into the tar pit like a bungee jumper. At the bottom of the pit was a pile of bones. Sid got trapped inside an ancient dinosaur skeleton when he touched down. He stayed trapped as the vine hoisted the skeleton high into the air!

Sid peeked out of his skeletal cage. The mini-sloths were screaming and running away.

There was no question—they were spooked!

"Bad juju!" one sloth shouted.

CHAPTER EIGHT

Boom!

Spurts of hot steam gushed out of the ground into the air. Giant trees toppled over. The sound of boiling water was earsplitting. They were surrounded by geysers!

"I'm too young to die!" Crash cried.

"Actually, possums have a short life span," Eddie said. "So you're kind of due."

Manny watched as more and more geysers exploded into the air. How would they get out of *this* mess?

"Guys!" Ellie's voice called. "Head out from the tree, pass three geysers, then go left!"

Manny glanced up. He saw Ellie perched on the branch of a redwood tree. "What are you doing up there?" he cried.

"The geysers are blowing in a pattern," Ellie said. "I can see it from here."

Freed from the vine, Sid landed on top of the giant statue just as it started to crumble. He was stripped of his bone and knocked out cold, and ended up floating down a stream on a broken plank of wood.

Meanwhile, his mammal friends were waking up to find themselves completely surrounded by . . .

"Water!!!" Diego cried.

"Crash, I told you not to drink before bed!" Eddie scolded.

"I didn't do this!" Crash exclaimed.

Manny looked around. The ice they had camped out on the night before had begun to melt.

"We need to move," Manny said.

"Wait," Diego said. "Where's Sid?"

"I am Fire-god!" a voice muttered. "Kneel at the altar of Sid!"

Out from the reeds drifted a piece of wood. Fast asleep on it was Sid!

"Sid, wake up!" Manny yelled.

"Huh?" Sid said. He sat up with a start. "What a night. I was kidnapped by a tribe of mini-sloths. They worshipped me!"

"You must have been dreaming!" Diego said.

Sid frowned as everyone guffawed. Why wouldn't his friends believe him?

The mammals hit the road again.

From the top of a muddy hill, they spotted a tall craggy mountain in the distance. Perched on its summit was a boat.

"There it is!" Diego exclaimed.

"We're going to make it!" Crash cried.

The group celebrated with an awesome mudball fight. But just as Sid was getting pummeled with a flurry of mudballs, the ground below gave way.

"Ahhhhhh!"

"Heeeeelp!"

"Whooooooa!"

The group plunged twenty feet before landing with a splat. They climbed out of muddy holes and looked around. They were surrounded by giant redwood trees.

And something else . . .

"Did the scary vulture say anything about exploding geysers?" Sid asked.

"No, why?" Manny asked.

Ellie promised to guide her friends through the exploding geyser field. She would then follow her own directions to safety.

"As you said, a mammoth never forgets." Ellie said.

Manny lifted the possums and Sid and placed them on his back. He wasn't crazy about Ellie's plan, but there was no other way. So with Diego behind them, Manny moved out.

"Go left!" Ellie directed. "Good! Now cut right! Awesome!"

The group zigzagged through the exploding maze. After a few close calls they were home free.

"You did it!" Ellie cheered. She was about to climb down from the tree when—

Boom! Boom! Boom!

Ellie froze. A bunch of geysers were exploding all around her!

"Oh, boy," Ellie groaned.

The tree underneath her burst into splinters. She had to get out of the field fast!

Ellie could hardly see through the thick mist. She could hear the guys cheering her on as she crisscrossed the exploding geysers.

Crash and Eddie ran to meet Ellie.

The ground rumbled and began to split. On one side of the deep crack stood Manny, Sid, and Diego. On the other side stood Ellie and the possums.

"We're okay!" Ellie called through the mist.

Manny stared at the crack. It was too deep for them to cross.

"Go around the mountain, Ellie!" Manny called. "We'll meet you at the boat!"

"Last one there is a fossil!" Ellie called back.

By now, boiling water was pouring through the canyon and heading for the dam.

"The worst is behind us," Manny said. "But it's catching up to us quickly."

Time was running out for the migrating mammals. Would they make it to the boat? Or would the raging flood waters halt them permanently?

CHAPTER NINE

"Stop pushing!"

"Keep it moving!"

"Quit tailgating!"

Hoards of edgy animals shouted as they pushed their way to the boat.

"Do not leave your children unattended," a vulture announced. "All unattended children will be eaten."

Manny searched for Ellie as he, Sid, and Diego squeezed through the crowd. "Has anyone seen a mammoth?" he asked around.

"Sure have!" a rhino answered.

"Where?" Manny asked excitedly.

"I'm looking at him!" the rhino said.

"No—not me!" Manny cried.

"Come on, Manny," Diego said. "Maybe Ellie is already on the boat."

But getting on the boat wasn't easy, thanks to a picky gatekeeper bird named Gustav.

"This is a preboarding announcement," Gustav shouted. "We are only boarding passengers with mates."

"What if we don't have a mate?" Sid cried.

"Then you must travel standby," Gustav said.

"What's standby travel?" Diego asked.

"You stand by—and we travel!" Gustav answered.

Suddenly the valley shook with tremors. Manny knew they had to get on the boat before the dam broke, or else.

"But what about you?" Manny demanded. "*You* don't have a mate!"

"But I *do* have power," Gustav bragged. "So whatever I say goes!"

That was a bad answer!

The animals glared at Gustav.

"Attention!" Manny shouted. "At this time we are boarding *everyone*!"

A stampede thundered up the boarding ramp.

"I'm in charge here!" Gustav shouted. "Me! Me!"

As Manny walked up the ramp he felt awful. Why hadn't Ellie and the possums shown up yet?

Just then a voice called out to him.

"Manny! Manny!"

Manny spun around. Crash and Eddie were racing toward the boat.

"It's Ellie!" Eddie shouted.

"She's trapped in a cave!" Crash cried.

CHAPTER TEN

Manny had to save Ellie.

He charged down the ramp. Then, with his friends following, he ran away from the boat and down the hill.

The trio ran faster and faster. But as they crossed a long ice-bridge, a giant wave knocked it in half.

Sid and Diego clung to one end of the bridge. Manny clung to the other. Crash and Eddie hugged a tree above the raging waters.

"Go save our sister, Manny!" Crash called.

"I'll save the possums!" Sid shouted.

He dove off of the ledge and crashed with a smack into an ice block. The possums watched as Sid floated facedown in the water.

"Who's going to save *him*?" Crash asked.

Diego knew it was up to him. He remembered what Sid taught him about swimming. Swimming was just like stalking!

Diego gathered his courage. It was either sink or swim—and he was going to swim!

Jump in . . . now! Diego told himself.

After a few brave tries, Diego plunged into the water. He cat-paddled the waves while chanting, "Claw, kick! Claw, kick!"

Diego reached Sid and the possums just as they went under. He took a deep breath and dove beneath the water. After a few seconds, Diego popped up with Sid between his teeth and the possums on his head!

Diego swam to shore and gently placed his friends on the riverbank.

"Nothing to it," Diego said. "Most animals *can* swim as babies!"

"Not tigers," Sid said. "I left that part out!"

Ellie was still in the cave, trapped by a fallen boulder. Water crashed over the boulder and into the cave. As the water rose higher and higher, Ellie took her last precious breaths.

At the same time Manny reached the end of the ice-bridge. He was about to step off when the ledge cracked. A block of ice plunged into a raging whirlpool—the same waters blocking Ellie's cave. Manny jumped into the whirlpool. He wrapped his trunk around a floating tree and jammed it into a space above the boulder.

Manny worked to pry the boulder out. Finally the boulder popped out, and the water spilled out of the cave. So did Ellie!

A cheer rose from the boat as everyone watched the daring rescue.

"Manny, look out!" Ellie shouted.

Manny felt himself dragged under the water.

There to greet him were Cretaceous and Maelstrom!

While Manny struggled with the reptiles, a little Scrat was struggling to stash his last acorn on dry land. He jammed the acorn into a glacier. The ice broke in half and—*Whoosh!* Tons of water was sucked into its deep crack. So were Cretaceous and Maelstrom!

Farther away, the escape boat rocked back and forth on its craggy pedestal. The animals screamed as a wave hit the boat and sent it plummeting to the ground.

Manny held onto a frozen boulder with his strong tusks. He waited until the water level dropped lower and lower. Soon Manny and the boat were resting on dry land. But where was Ellie?

The passengers on the boat cheered as Ellie stepped out of the cave.

"This is our final destination," Gustav announced. "Please exit in an orderly fashion."

The animals stampeded over Gustav's back. They gazed out at the dry valley dotted with sparkling lakes. It was the most awesome sight they had seen in a long time.

"About the swimming tips, Sid," Diego said. "You've got my respect, buddy."

Sid smiled as he wiped his nose with his furry arm.

"And just like that you take it away!" Diego growled.

A loud trumpeting sound blared.

Manny's jaw dropped. A parade of mammoths were marching around the bend. Manny and Ellie were *not* the last mammoths on earth after all!

Ellie lumbered after the herd. "Aren't you coming, Manny?" she called.

"You want to go with them?" Manny asked.

"I am a mammoth," Ellie decided. "So I really should go with them, right?"

Manny didn't know what to do. He wanted to be with Ellie more than anything. At the same time, he didn't want to leave his friends and the memory of his family.

Manny hung his big woolly head and said, "Good-bye, Ellie. I hope you find what you're looking for."

"Good-bye, Manny," Ellie said softly. Then she turned and joined the herd with Crash and Eddie.

Manny was still gazing after Ellie when a breeze rippled a puddle at his feet. When the water stilled, the images of his wife and son appeared. With love in her eyes, Manny's wife nodded "good-bye." After that, the image disappeared.

In a flash Manny got it. His family was giving him permission to get a life—a brand-new life.

"Go after her," Sid said.

"We'll always be here for you," Diego said.

"I'll keep in touch!" Manny said as he walked faster and faster toward the herd.

"Ellie! Ellie!" he called.

Ellie turned in the middle of the herd. She could hear Manny, but where was he?

Crash and Eddie pointed upward. Ellie glanced up and gasped. Manny was hanging from a branch by his tail!

"I want to be with you, Ellie!" Manny pleaded. "What do you say?"

"I'm in!" Ellie said.

Manny was ten tons of sheer joy as he dropped from the tree. The two mammoths joined trunks. Then together they joined their friends.

"What about your herd?" Diego asked.

Manny picked Sid up and placed him on his back. "This *is* our herd!" he said.

"Lead the way, Diego!" Sid declared.

The happy travelers made their way into the sunset. Not so happy were Cretaceous and Maelstrom. Their lifeless bodies were being carried off by the tribe of mini-sloths!

"Bad juju?" one sloth asked.

"Good sushi!" another one answered.

The reptiles were prehistoric history—but the mammals of the world had plenty to celebrate. The Ice Age would survive—and so would they.